the SMURFS™

MEET SMURFETTE

by Peyo

Simon Spotlight

New York   London   Toronto   Sydney

SIMON SPOTLIGHT

An imprint of Simon & Schuster Children's Publishing Division

1230 Avenue of the Americas, New York, New York 10020

© Peyo - 2003 - Licensed through Lafig Belgium - www.smurf.com

English language translation copyright © 2011 by Peyo - Licensed through Lafig Belgium - www.smurf.com.

All rights reserved. All rights reserved, including the right of reproduction in whole or in part in any form.

SIMON SPOTLIGHT and colophon are registered trademarks of Simon & Schuster, Inc.

For information about special discounts for bulk purchases, please contact Simon & Schuster Special Sales at 1-866-506-1949 or business@simonandschuster.com.

Manufactured in the United States of America 0411 LAK

First Edition 10 9 8 7 6 5 4 3 2 1

ISBN 978-1-4424-2290-2

It was late at night, but Gargamel, the evil wizard, was still hard at work. He was clearly up to something . . .

"If I just add a few crocodile tears, a viper's tongue, and a touch of finch brain to this blue clay . . . ," Gargamel muttered. "Aha! This time I'll get you, you miserable elves!"

Gargamel was working on his latest plan to capture the Smurfs!

The next day the Smurfs were busy gathering food for the winter. They had to stock enough chestnuts, walnuts, and hazelnuts to feed them until spring.

Just then one Smurf heard a very strange, high-pitched noise. It sounded like someone was sobbing. He walked toward the noise and found a strange creature in the middle of a clearing . . .

"Who are you?" asked the Smurf.

"I am a Smurfette!" she answered.

"Are you? I've never seen one! And why are you smurfing so much?" he asked.

"Because I'm all alone and have nowhere to go," she replied.

"Well, you can smurf back to the village with me!" he offered.

"Oh, thank you," said the Smurfette. "But I'm so tired. Can you carry me?"

"Umm . . . okay," he said, as he threw her over his shoulder like a sack of potatoes.

When Smurfette arrived in Smurf village, all of the Smurfs crowded around to get a closer look, and laughed when they heard her shrill voice. They had never seen a Smurfette before.

They gave Smurfette her own mushroom house to live in, and let her decorate it however she wanted. The Smurfs were a little surprised by her choice of paint colors, but she seemed so sad when they suggested changing it that they simply followed her orders.

Unfortunately the Smurfs had no idea that Smurfette wasn't a real Smurf at all. Gargamel created her out of blue clay and sent her to Smurf village. He wanted Smurfette to trick the Smurfs into following her back to his cottage, and talked to her through her magical powder compact.

"Don't forget," said Gargamel. "If you make them fall in love with you, they'll do anything you want!"

But that was no easy task. Even though the Smurfs wanted to give Smurfette a warm welcome, they thought she was too friendly. They weren't even that excited when she invited them all to a big picnic.

On the day of the picnic Smurfette waited for her guests—but nobody came. Nobody, except Jokey Smurf . . . who was nice enough to bring her a gift! Unfortunately it was an exploding package as usual.

Smurfette was furious. She gave up trying to win the Smurfs over. Being nice wasn't working! It was time for plan B.

Smurfette made her way to the dam over the Smurf River. She was going to try to flood Smurf village. If she succeeded, maybe Gargamel would forgive her for not making the Smurfs fall in love with her.

On the footbridge of the dam, Smurfette found Greedy Smurf standing by himself.

"This dam is magnificent," she told Greedy, "but what do you do when the lake overflows?"

"Well, we smurf the gate to let some water out," Greedy answered.

Smurfette smiled. "If I give you this cake, will you show me how it's done?" she asked.

"Uh, okay," Greedy said, "but just for a second!"

Greedy pushed the lever and the water rushed out of the gate of the dam. But when he was about to shut the gate, Smurfette held down the lever.

"Are you crazy?" shouted the Smurf. "Do you want to flood the village?"

"Yes!" yelled Smurfette.

Soon the water that had been flowing peacefully over the rocks turned into a fast-moving river.

"Oh, no!" cried the Smurfs. "The dam must have smurfed!"

Greedy tried hard to push Smurfette away from the lever. Finally she fell into the river, and the current quickly swept her away. She yelled for help as loudly as she could, but no one could hear her.

Luckily for Smurfette, some Smurfs spotted her on their way to the dam. Holding hands, they formed a chain and were able to pull her out of the rapids.

The Smurfs closed the gate of the dam, and the water level slowly went down. The Smurfs were so angry with Smurfette. Papa Smurf decided that she needed to be punished for what she had done.

"Smurfette," said Papa Smurf, "why did you try to flood the village?"

Smurfette thought for a moment and then started to sob. "I don't know," she said, "You've been so good to me . . . but Gargamel created me and he smurfs my actions! Oh, how I would love to be a real Smurfette: kind and happy like all of you!"

The Smurfs weren't angry anymore. They felt sorry for her.

"Hmm," said Papa Smurf. "I might be able to smurf something . . ."

In his laboratory Papa Smurf covered Smurfette with all kinds of potions, hoping to turn her into a real Smurfette. All the Smurfs waited outside, and when the door of the lab finally opened, Papa Smurf walked out with a big smile on his face.

"I think I've succeeded!" he said. "And the result is totally smurfing!"

He was right! Smurfette had changed completely. She was no longer the evil Smurfette they had met. All the Smurfs fell in love with her on the spot.

Before long, Smurfette couldn't go anywhere without a crowd of Smurfs around her. They brought her gifts, and fought over who got to talk with her first.

Papa Smurf shook his head. "I wonder," he said, "if this Smurfette is about to smurf us more problems than the first one. . . ."